Exit, Stage Left

Exit, Stage Left

A TIME TRAVEL ROMANCE NOVELETTE

ERIN KRUEGER

BARTIE BOOKS

First Edition

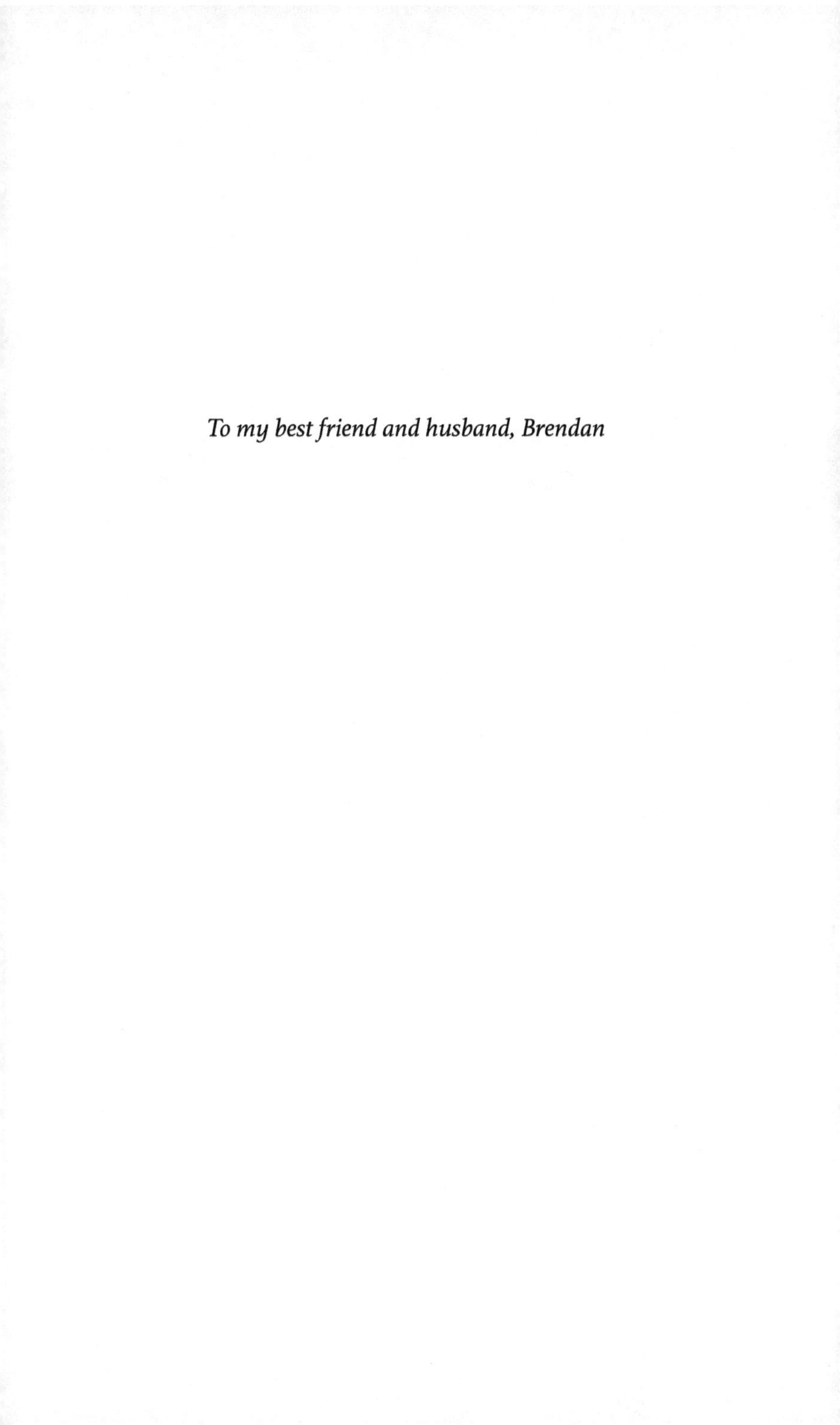

To my best friend and husband, Brendan

Chapter One

Opening night of the brand-new Regency farce, *The Adventures of Mr. Bingley's Other Friend*, was less than twenty-four hours away. As head props and costumes manager, Wren Dynamene *should* have been more worried about the performance. But it was her surprise birthday celebration she dreaded more.

As if on cue, a stagehand carrying a large white bakery box entered from the wings and slipped behind the parlor backdrop.

Wren's gut clenched, but she willed it away. Another stagehand crossed the stage holding balloons, sneaking behind the backdrop.

Was it too late to escape the fuss and attention?

Wren closed her eyes. Yes. The only thing that would stop this troupe of community theater actors from throwing a party would be if Jane Austen herself appeared and commented on their *sparkling* performance. Still, nothing was impossible where the stage was concerned. It was as if there was a bit of leftover magic from days past hanging like a sheer cloud backstage. And more than once Wren had caught sight of "ghosts" during late night runs.

"There you are."

Wren spun.

"Hey Mar—" Her breath caught at the sight of the lead actor, and her best friend, Marco Manzanares. In a red t-shirt and dark jeans—wow. Hot as a desert summer. She cleared her throat and focused on releasing her talon grip on the clipboard one finger at a time. If Marco ever found out she'd been crushing on him since, oh, *forever*, he'd be mortified.

"You dropped this." He bent to pick up her pen and she got a whiff of him. Fresh. Not too much. Cool water and calm pools. But that did nothing to quell her racing pulse. He stood and held it out to her, his eyes twinkling. "Don't want to lose it."

Wren took the pen, her fingers brushing his. That was not helping. Not helping at all. She just had to act normal and slow the thudding in her chest.

"Thanks." She gave him a small smile and tucked the pen into her bun where her auburn curls would hold the traitorous object prisoner. See, she could do it. Her hands only shook mildly.

"All this..." She gestured to the stage. "Why not just a quick 'happy birthday' in passing, and then we can go home?"

"I tried talking to them, but they insisted." His apologetic brown gaze met hers and something flip-flopped inside her. "Just think of it as a few minutes in front of your friends. And then you can do whatever you want afterwards."

"Like sleep?"

"If that's your birthday wish, then yes. Oh, and I baked your favorite cupcakes. We'll swing by my place to get them when I drop you home. *If* you suffer through five minutes of birthday cake and song."

"You made me spice cake?" He never baked for anyone.

"With cream cheese frosting and no raisins."

Wren took a deep breath. "Okay. For the cupcakes."

"For the cupcakes." He offered his arm to escort her behind the backdrop. As soon as the grinning performers and stage crew saw her, they began singing "Happy Birthday" in an eight-part chorus, complete with seventh ring harmony. It should've warmed her heart, but all she could think about was fleeing the over-the-top attention.

Wren knew what they expected, what she had to do, even if being center stage had her insides feeling like jelly. She'd once been a lead actress herself before that horrid night. So, pasting a smile on her face, Wren blew a kiss to everyone.

"Thank you, really," she said. The most brightly colored frosted cake she'd ever seen, with four flickering, mismatched candles, was placed before her.

"Make a wish," someone shouted. The whole group cheered.

"For the cupcakes," Marco whispered at her side. Wren met his gaze, and he gave her arm an encouraging pat. It was then that she realized she was still gripping his arm, hadn't let him go. She released her hand and nodded. A wish.

She glanced up and found Marco. He'd meandered into the group and now stood across from her. Sparks charged up her spine as their eyes met. That look could've lit up the stage. He winked, and her cheeks burned in response. If she truly wished for what she wanted...

But she couldn't. Could she?

Maybe one day she'd get the courage. For now, she'd just go with something quick, what everyone wished for. Love and courage, right?

She took a deep breath and blew out the candles. One exhale and it was over. As she took in the crowd, Marco had his eyes closed. Had he also made a wish? Now she was being ridiculous. No one made wishes on other people's birthday cakes. Especially not on their milestone twenty-fifth birthday.

From somewhere behind her, a breeze blew in, setting every single one of her arm hairs on edge. She swore time slowed just slightly, as if a clock's second hand had stuttered over its ticking. Nothing more, nothing less. But for a brief moment, everyone moved slower, clapping in discordant sounds, jarring her ears. Their movements as they began to mingle seemed to be out of sync with the rest of the room and then, as if they were given a prompt, they all sped up to catch up to the correct time. Arm hairs tingling, Wren brushed them down and glanced around the group. She was imagining things. Had to be. No one else had seemed to notice.

Except Marco.

Chapter Two

He stood staring at her, his brown eyes wide and unblinking. "What just happened?" he mouthed, then brushed at his arms.

The cast took the pause as a cue to circle around her, closing in, suffocating her. All eyes focused on her, waiting for her to say something more. Wren started shaking. Her throat turned to dust.

"Cake time everyone." Marco stepped up to the table. "Come grab a slice."

She breathed a sigh of relief. "Thank you," she mouthed. He nodded.

"Where's Wren?" someone shouted above the din. "The costume and props manager. Where is she?"

"Over there," the second understudy of Lord Steffington said around a mouthful of cake. He pointed to Wren with his now empty fork. The uncharacteristically frazzled assistant director hustled toward her.

"I've been texting you for the last half hour, but this place is a black hole for service. We have a sword, right?" the woman asked, her glasses threatening to fall from their perch on her head.

"I'm sure we do, but I was told we had everything for the play." Wren raised a brow. Especially since she was now having to do two jobs, props manager *and* costumes manager, since Evelyn quit. Sometimes Wren thought being an actor would've been so much easier.

"There's been a last-minute change. The director says the Colonel needs it for 'character development.'"

"I'll go right now." Wren scurried away, happy for an excuse to leave. But a sword? The Colonel already had a hook for a hand. Did the director want the character to have two peg legs next? Why not commit to the theme and make him a pirate colonel?

"Hey, wait up," Marco called after her.

"I won't be long." She hurried down the corridor, past the green room, and opened the heavy steel doors to the wardrobe at the end of the hall. She wove her way expertly through the space, searching through decades of acquired costumes and props for a rubber cutlass she was sure they had.

A rustle. Wren paused, ears straining towards the sound. There it was again. Near the back of the room. Probably a mouse. They'd have to call an exterminator in before the little rodent chewed through all the costumes. And left lovely pellets in the hats. Wren groaned. Why couldn't they have more than a flickering fluorescent light above? Wasn't bright light supposed to keep the critters at bay?

But the rustling sounded again, and Wren's very core went on high alert.

"Hello?" She shoved more garments aside and spied the cutlass lying in a metal basket with other random weapons. She grabbed it. "Who's in here?"

Suit coats on a clothing rack next to her shifted and a tall, slender, middle-aged woman, wearing a white cap and mint green empire waist gown, passed between them. A squeak escaped Wren's lips before she could recover herself. Wren pointed the rubber weapon at the stranger, watching as pale blue smoke created a mist around the costumed woman.

"Ah, there you are," the woman said in a British accent and smiled.

Wren stepped back. "Who are you?"

"I'm Miss Austen."

"Miss Austen? Do you mean Jane Austen?"

The woman nodded.

"But we already have one. And she only provides the monologue at the beginning and end of the play. Hold on. Did our director put you up to this?" She'd kill him. It was one thing to make a colonel a pirate, but to add an entirely new character to the performance the night before it went on was just plain stupid.

Their current Jane, with waist length pink hair and silver nose ring, didn't look anything like the woman standing before her. Miss Austen held Wren with rich hazel eyes and a face that could have been painted on a porcelain doll, so delicate and refined as it was. Dark brown hair peeked out from beneath the woman's mob cap and curled against her round cheeks. She was striking, and Wren couldn't help but feel awe at the sight of her. In fact, if they replaced "Jane" with the "Miss Austen" who had appeared out of thin air, it seemed, it might lend their performance some sorely missing authenticity.

"Why are you here? I mean, here in the wardrobe?" Wren managed to ask at last.

"My dear, you summoned me. You are Miss Dynamene, are you not?"

"You know my name?" Wren cocked a brow.

"Indeed. The last time I was summoned thusly, I walked into a space called a 'nightclub' where women in the most scandalous attire I'd ever beheld danced before my own eyes. So much beading and fringe." The woman shook her head, frowning.

"And you," she clicked her tongue and appraised her. "Aide you with love? If you desire assistance in that regard, we shall have to discuss the matter. For I am uncertain why a capable young woman as yourself should not know her own mind. But in matters of the heart, love is a fickle beast. And in one moment it may well change your views to another."

"I—" Wren blinked, trying to think. Why was Jane there? It made no sense. And yet there was an air about this one as if she believed herself to *actually be* Miss Austen.

The cake. Her wish.

Wren's eyes flew wide.

"I summoned you," she said quietly, her brain finally clicking the pieces together. "You're really Miss Austen. As in *the* Jane Austen. Not an actor here for the play?"

"Good heavens, no. Allow me a newly sharpened quill and some ink, and I shall write you a script better than anything I could perform."

"If that's who you say you are, tell me, is—?" Wren bit her lip, thinking of anything that could be a small trivia factoid only Jane herself might know. She smiled when she thought of it. "Is Mr. Darcy in *Pride and Prejudice* based on your lover, Mr. Tom Lefroy, or someone else?"

Jane's jaw dropped. Then she composed herself immediately. "Mr. Lefroy and I were quite close, yes. And there was a time I fancied myself quite in love with the man. But no. How came you to that knowledge? I only wrote of him to my sister, Cassandra."

"I know a lot of things?" Wren shrugged. It wasn't lying, exactly.

"As to the other question, of Mr. Darcy, he is more modeled after my own countenance. Mr. Lefroy has a much more open and pleasing spirit."

"So he was your inspiration for Elizabeth Bennet, then."

"In some ways, perhaps he was." Jane's gaze took on a faraway look.

"Anything new you're working on?" Wren asked, hooking the sword on a finger, and poking through the hanging suits with her spare hand. Believing a historical figure had miraculously appeared in the present— Well, that took the cake. And where had the blue smoke come from? She waved it away.

"At present, I am occupied with another novel. One where I fear only I will enjoy the heroine," the authoress said. A tiny line formed between her dark brows.

If Wren had any doubts left, they vanished as she watched Jane. She'd seen that look before in a drawing. Same grimacing expression. Same deep-set gaze. Same crossed arms. The sketch of the authoress had truly come to life.

A loud crash near the front of the room made Wren jump, dropping the weapon.

"*Par dieu. Encore?*" A teenager, clad in white medieval armor and short bobbed hair, pushed toward them through a rack of women's floral dresses. She swatted at her chest and little puffs of pale blue smoke faded into the ether.

All three of them stared at each other. The seconds ticked by. Wren couldn't move.

"Well, someone better offer me a *café*," the teen said in near-perfect English. "This is the fifth, *non*, sixth time I have been sent to the future this month and I need the caffeine."

"I'm sorry, what?" Wren asked.

"Jehanne D'Arc," she said with an elegant bow. "Ah, a sword." She picked up the rubber cutlass.

Wren looked to Jane. She raised her hands as if to say she didn't know.

"You *have* heard of me, *non*?"

"I—" Wren began.

"Call me Joan," the young woman said with an exasperated sigh. "You wished for courage to help with your love, *oui*? *Et voilà!* I have come. I do not know what is ailing the future, but there seems to be a considerable lack of courage." She tugged her finger over the tip of the sword and scowled as it bent.

"Thank you," Wren said. Okay, so her wish had sent two people to the future now. Two vastly different women. She could handle that, right? There was no denying the young lady before her was Joan of Arc. More unbelievable was the fact that Wren felt more certain of her realness than she had been of Jane Austen.

"*Bon.* So, who is the person you need help with?" Joan asked and then pointed the weapon at a spot over Wren's shoulder. "Maybe...him?"

Wren turned to find Marco, a confused expression on his handsome face, standing in the open wardrobe doorway. He held a paper plate with a large slice of birthday cake resting on it.

She nodded.

"*Parfait.*" Joan patted her on the back.

Chapter Three

"Marco, you followed me." Wren hurried over to him.

"I got you a slice, since you had to cut out so––"

"Whoa, Mama. Look out," a male's voice bellowed from behind her.

Wren spun, knocking Marco's plate onto the front of her favorite yellow t-shirt. A dollop of neon rainbow icing plopped to the floor, just missing the toe of her black Chucks.

From an empty clothing rack, a man appeared out of yet another mist of blue smoke. Seriously, where was the smoke coming from? He coughed and smacked at his white Western shirt and black pants. Tendrils of the vapor stretched away from him.

"Oh jeez, Wren. Your shirt." Marco reached to brush her off. Wren froze. Would he touch her? Was it bad of her to hope he would?

Marco paused, hand in mid-air. He reddened to the tips of his ears.

"Don't worry about it." Wren swiped the icing clinging to her shirt and dropped the mess and her disappointment onto the plate. Marco handed her the tiniest cocktail napkin she'd ever seen, and she cleaned her fingers the best she could, then wiped up the icing on the floor.

"How're we doin' tonight? Elvis Presley. A pleasure it is to meet you, honey," the stranger said with a velvety Southern drawl.

"I *know* I didn't wish for this," she muttered after she'd stated her name.

"Marco Manzanares." Marco jutted out a hand for the King and shook it heartily.

If she was going to have time-traveling people, one weird historical person was fine. Two, sure. But three? "Why is this happening?"

"You know, it's funny. I could've sworn I was just going into a photo session for '*Blue Hawaii*' when *blammo*, I'm here in... Uh, honey, where exactly am I?" The man hooked a thumb in his beltloop, looking around.

"Elvis, huh?" Marco said. Wren waited for the knowledge to hit Marco.

One second. Two.

Marco's eyes widened. "You mean, literally? *The* Elvis. Like, as in, *The King*. Not an impersonator."

"Appears so," Wren said. "And she's Jane Austen. And she's Joan of Arc."

"You're kidding." He laughed, scanning the trio anew.

"Mr. Presley, you are, as we all are, in what appears to be some sort of large dressing room, caring for the needs of our friend." Jane deigned to glance his way and Elvis gave her a wink. She scowled in return.

"*En garde!*" Joan pointed the sword at him.

Oh, good God. These three were going to be the death of each other before Wren had even figured out how to get them back to where they came from.

"Jane and Joan said I brought them here when I wished on my cake," Wren said. She wiped a still-sticky hand on the thigh of her blue jeans. "Promise you won't say anything? Not until I can—"

"Where the heck is she?" The director burst into the costume room, angry. "She's been gone nearly twenty—"

The stunned trio of time travelers stared at the director, mouths agape. Marco froze like a deer in headlights. Wren wanted to curl up into a ball in a dark corner and forget all of what happened.

"You." The director's gaze speared Wren then slid to Joan. "Ah, I see you found the sword."

Joan raised a brow and the sword at the same time. "This is a sword?" She scoffed.

"Place that with the colonel's props. Then get out, all of you. I'm locking up."

Who was going to take care of the new strangers? Okay, not technically strangers now. But still, they couldn't sleep at the theater. With a sinking feeling in Wren's gut, the only logical answer was they were her responsibility now.

"Just leaving." Wren wanted to add "aye, aye," but thought it might not be the best response. She shepherded the time-traveling trio out. "Marco, where are we going to take them? They'll be crammed in like sardines in my studio apartment."

"What about a hotel?" he offered.

"I can't afford that." Especially when she considered they'd have to get more than one room. Not on her meager salary. Props and costumes didn't exactly pay for hotel suites. And no way was she leaving Elvis alone with Jane.

"Hmm." Marco stopped just outside the theater. "Okay, so I'll need an extra pair of hands, you know, to help me with all the time travelers, but there's always my place. I've got food, a sofa, blankets. The works."

Her insides liquified at the idea of spending the night in his roomy apartment. "You sure?"

"Positive. Plus, you need a change of clothes." He pointed to the smear of icing on her shirt.

"Those cupcakes you mentioned better not be a lie." She playfully bumped his shoulder with her own. "Thanks."

The next twenty minutes were spent convincing Jane that Marco's car didn't need horses and telling Elvis that seatbelts were, in fact, absolutely necessary. Joan had pantomimed what could happen if he didn't wear it, to Wren's amusement.

"Here we are." Marco pulled his SUV into a spot in front of his apartment complex. Two red brick-faced stories with white trim greeted them. He hopped out of the car and hurried to the door.

Jane tapped Wren's shoulder. "Mr. Manzanares is quite an excellent driver of this...barouche. And you could do worse than setting your cap at such a man as he. Why, look at the size of his home and all those windows! He must make more than a thousand pounds a year."

Wren shook her head. "We're just friends."

"This is why you made your wish. The man obviously cares about you, to support you and your guests in his home. Add to it that he provided you with delectable refreshments. I see your predicament," Jane said.

"Like I said. We're just good friends. It's too much to risk—"

"You're afraid to take the chance," Joan said from the backseat. "But what if he feels the same?"

"Is that why you all came? To help me and Marco?" Wren unclipped her seatbelt. "I have other things you could help with. Other things needing courage."

"Bah. This is the hardest task," Joan said. "When I heard that wish through time, I could not keep from answering it. Like a lost animal crying into the mist."

"I did *not* cry." Wren pursed her lips.

"My dear, the depth of your need was too much to ignore. Very compelling," Jane added.

Wren's gaze caught movement outside the car. Marco was waving them all in from the door of his apartment building.

"Hold on. Wren made a wish?" Elvis asked. "All I heard was—"

"Okay, everyone out." Wren hustled everyone out of the car and into Marco's apartment before she had to answer.

Marco greeted her at the entrance. "I'll show you to my room."

Wren raised her brows.

"I mean, in my dresser I have extra tees so you can, uh, change." He rubbed the back of his neck. "Take all the time you need. Or be as quick as you like. I'll entertain the group in the meantime."

"Thanks." She'd never seen Marco so flustered and nervous.

"Second drawer," he said and hopped over the back of the couch to sit next to Elvis.

Such an extrovert, she thought to herself, chuckling. Marco always loved being in the limelight. At one point she liked it, too. But if you're always in front, all your faults are visible.

Wren shrugged the thought away and went to Marco's room, closing the door behind her. His cologne wafted to greet her. Wren couldn't help but take in a big whiff of it.

No. Bad Wren. Clothes.

His room was spotless without being sterile, furnished with a dark wooden dresser and bed frame and a green plaid duvet. With windows on three walls, the room would be airy and bright in the daytime. But at that time of night, hundreds of stars filled the view. Awestruck, she almost wished...

No. Wishing already had unintended consequences. Focus.

T-shirt. She needed a new t-shirt. And Marco only hung up his button-downs. She tugged the top dresser drawer open.

"Omigosh." Wren slammed it shut again. She shook her head hoping to rid herself of the image. But that pair of highlighter-green boxer briefs emblazoned with awkward winky faces staring back at her would forever be etched in her brain. So, he was an emojis guy?

Curiosity got the better of her and she pulled the handle to open it again. The next pair was patterned with swirling bright purple monster faces, tongue out and everything. Classic Marco. But the sight of something red and fuzzy poking out from beneath the stack of boxer briefs made her pause. She lifted the corner and... Her eyes widened.

Handcuffs.

He seriously had red fuzzy handcuffs.

Oh, he was *never* going to hear the end of that.

Snickering to herself, she closed the top drawer and opened the one below it. There were all the t-shirts. She grabbed the one on top. But it was a struggle to remove her stained shirt without smearing more frosting everywhere. And then, how could she not nuzzle the soft fabric of Marco's gray one as it went over her head? How did they make men's t-shirts so soft? What would it feel like on him? Maybe he'd hold her in his arms where she could press a cheek to his chest. They could lean closer and—

Wren caught a glance of herself in his closet mirror. Disappearing in his oversized t-shirt, always behind the scenes of performances, hiding in the shadows. Who was she compared to the leading man?

She picked up her dirty top, took a deep breath, and left the room.

Chapter Four

"Look okay?" she asked, finding all of them in the living room. Marco turned from chatting with Elvis, a smile on his lips. At the sight of her, his brows lifted.

"Much better on you than it ever was on me," he said. She seriously doubted that.

"Where should I put this?" Wren held up her bundle of soiled shirt.

"I'll just throw that in the wash." His hand touched hers as he took it, warmth spreading up her arm.

"Thanks." She smiled, then turned before he could see her blush.

"Hey, Marco, my main man, why don't we get this party rockin'?" The King, a puzzled look on his face, stood in front of the sixty-inch screen with a music app open on it. "How do you get it to play records?"

Joan rolled her eyes and handed him the remote. "You need this."

"I choose 'Jailhouse Rock'," Marco said.

"Or," Wren said, quickly hiding every remote in the room. "Or we could rehearse your lines, Marco?"

The last thing anyone needed was a squawking fifties serenade from Marco, or Elvis judo-chopping and breaking something. On further thought, why was Elvis even there—moral support? Distraction? Hair care tips? She shrugged it off.

"Good call. Elvis, raincheck."

The King gave Marco a thumbs up. "Stay cool, kid," he said before heading to the kitchen.

Marco rushed off to his room and returned with a spare script.

"You be Lady Amelia," he said.

"Oh no. I'll be the butler."

"No. I need help with the fainting scene. I don't know what to do with these." He lifted his palms.

"Your hands?"

"Yeah, she faints, but every time... Here, just faint into my arms. I'll show you."

Wren stared at the pages. "There's nothing like that in the script."

"No?" Marco furrowed his brow. "Swore there was. Maybe it was the director's change in rehearsal tonight."

"I know this play backwards and forwards. Lady Amelia says, 'Oh Lord Steffington, what-*evah* shall I do?' and then she bats her eyes and—"

"I have never heard anyone from England sound like that," Jane said, pressing fingertips to her forehead before leaving the room.

Wren frowned.

"She's right," Marco said. "Lady Amelia does sound like a horrible Scarlett O'Hara. Just be you. I wish you would've applied for the part. Or even the understudy. No one's taken it yet. You'd make a much better Lady Amelia than—"

"I'm perfectly happy working backstage. Props and costumes are my comfort zone. Too much chance of me ruining a show if I'm out in the limelight. You remember what happened."

She'd been the female lead and her boyfriend at the time was the male lead. They were onstage together just before the final curtain. She had four lines to say, but she'd forgotten the last line. Panicking, she glanced at him for help and all he did was smirk as he waited for her to finish. The cast in the wings urged her on. Her chest tightened. She couldn't remember the line. The curtain wouldn't fall until she'd said it. Someone in the audience coughed. The silence went on for what seemed like hours. Someone in the audience had started laughing, and soon everyone was, even her boyfriend. The stage manager, exasperated, called for the curtain. As soon as it dropped, she'd fled the stage, vowing never to put herself in that place again.

Marco touched her arm, and she shook her head, returning to the present.

"Wren, that was four years ago, and that guy was a jerk. You don't leave your partner hanging when they flub a line. I'm glad you broke up with him."

Wren didn't deserve Marco's kindness. She'd never told him that her *ex* was the one to break up with *her* after the final curtain, claiming that he couldn't be with someone who couldn't remember four measly lines and made him look bad.

"Yeah, well." She snorted. "What is it they say about elephants and actors?"

"That fear never looks good on either," he said quietly.

"Let's get back to the lines." She cleared her throat and became her version of Lady Amelia, no accidental Southern accent. "Lord Steffington, what would you have me do? I cannot go to Mr. Bingley's ball with Katherine still unwell at home."

"And now you faint," Marco whispered. He held out his arms in front of her.

"Wait. There's a sofa onstage." Wren pivoted, dramatically falling onto his couch instead, hand draped over her forehead. "Kneel next to me and place your hand behind my shoulders. Fan me with a shawl or something."

Marco knelt, slowly sliding a hand around her back, lifting her from the sofa toward him. "Like this?" His face was close, his brown eyes, fringed with impossibly dark lashes, locked on hers, his large hand pressed warm against her.

Joan's words came back to her: *What if he feels the same?*

Wren closed her eyes.

Soft lips touched hers. The barest hint of pressure, like gossamer wings. The fluttering in her stomach moved to a blacksmith's hammer in her chest. Barely a second, that was all, before a dish clattered to the kitchen floor. She jolted, and the arm that was so effortlessly draped over her head seconds ago shot downward, her elbow striking his cheek with a solid blow.

He cried out in pain. In one swift motion, he pulled her off the sofa as he rose, her tailbone smacking hard against the wooden floors. "Oh crap, sorry, Wren."

Stunned, Wren opened her eyes, but Marco was gone.

Chapter Five

Jane and Joan entered the living room as he disappeared into the kitchen.

"Is everything settled? Did you ask him?" Jane asked.

"Does a kiss that may have only been my imagination count?" she whispered, fingers touching her tingling lips.

Jane patted her knee. "Go talk to him."

"I can't. I'm still shaking." He'd kissed her, right? She hadn't dreamt it. But what if it wasn't anything at all? Only a stage kiss. Her heart dropped. He wouldn't be kissing her, just Lady Amelia. Jealousy attempted to rear its ugly head, but Wren stomped it down, telling herself it didn't matter.

"Shaking. So?" Joan hopped onto the sofa next to Wren. "It's not like you're going into battle and need a steady arm."

"I...can't." Wren fidgeted with the blanket.

Joan groaned and gestured to the TV. "*Bon.* The last time I was here, I saw *Pride and Prejudice.* Never finished past Mr. Collins and his proposal to Elizabeth. I need to know what happens next. *Tu sais?*"

"My novel is now a performance?" Jane knit her brows together.

"Many times over." Wren got up. "Remotes are over there." Any excuse to not think about the kiss-that-really-wasn't. Thankfully, Marco and Elvis weren't in the kitchen, but considering the man-crush her best friend had on The King, she was sure he was with him somewhere. Where they were, she didn't care. Right then, Wren needed a moment to recover herself. Nothing like giving the one you like an elbow to the face. A movie was a good idea. No one had to talk during it.

The plate of her birthday spice cupcakes called to her, and she ate one—heavenly—as she searched the cabinets for corn kernels and oil. She finished off the cupcake and grabbed the plastic jar.

"Hey," Marco said from behind.

Wren dropped the kernels. Immediately she crouched and bonked heads with him doing the same.

He laughed, picking up a kernel from under the stove. "You're dangerous."

"Apparently. Look, about what happened in there. I'm–"

"No, I should apologize. I dropped you."

"It's fine. It was an accident. You took my elbow to your face."

Marco laughed and rubbed his jaw. "Good thing we're friends, then."

She reached for a cluster of kernels to hide her disappointment.

Marco did too. His fingers brushed hers. Both of them paused, hands midair.

Friends.

Right. She needed to remember that.

Wren pulled her hand back, using it to tuck a bunch of curls behind her ear instead. "So, about that scene. I didn't realize there was a kiss in it."

"The director added that today."

"Another change. Where was I when this happened?" How dare her voice betray the hurt she felt. Lord Steffington making out with Lady Amelia onstage. What was the director thinking?

"You were backstage. His directions were to the actors. Last minute. Like the sword."

He was right. She wasn't an actor. What happened under the lights for the scenes didn't really apply to her so long as the costumes and props didn't need changing. Still, it shouldn't have stung as much as it did.

"Is our Lady Amelia a good—"

"Don't go there, Wren." Marco scooped up the kernels and threw them out. He stood and exhaled, facing away. No one spoke. Not her, not Marco, not the time traveling trio. He finally opened the fridge. "Want a Coke?"

"Sure." Convo over. And what a mess she'd made of it. Wren got out the pot and lid and made the popcorn. Just as it finished Elvis leaned on the counter beside her.

"The last time I had popcorn I had to offer it to this chick in a movie. Didn't even get to eat it. I'll just take this out to the rest of the folks." His eyes brightened as he grabbed the bowl of popcorn.

"Come on," Marco said. "They're starting the movie."

Wren followed him into the living room. The only two spots left were right next to each other on the couch. Jane looked at Wren innocently. Joan grinned and took a portion of popcorn to her seat on the floor. Elvis gave them an eyebrow waggle. Seriously, why was he even there?

"Ladies first." Marco gestured to the cushion.

They settled in, and when the old cushion slumped her toward him, she found herself pressed up against his shoulders.

"Sorry," she said, and nervously pushed herself off. "I can move."

"It's fine, as long as you don't mind."

Was he kidding? Pressed up against the guy she liked, who smelled amazing? Oh no, anything but *that*. Even if they were still only just friends, she would enjoy the closeness.

The movie started and immediately there was a disgruntled snort from Jane on the floor.

"What have they done to my words? This is an abomination of my work. They never said that in a rainstorm. He visits her at the Collins's home while they are out."

"I recommend you don't watch *Lost in Austen*, then," Wren said. Marco placed his arm along the back of the sofa behind Wren.

"I dunno. Are you sure they're still speaking English?" Elvis asked. "Who ardently confesses things?"

"Some people might," Marco said under his breath.

Wren caught him glancing around the room out of the corner of her eye. It could've only been more cliché if he'd started whistling.

And then the whistling began.

Her lips cracked in a half smile. Maybe that kiss hadn't been as staged as she thought.

"*Silence.* I'm waiting for the duel." Joan hugged her knees, captivated by the screen.

"I am afraid to disappoint you, but I never wrote a duel in the work. Though it would have been quite understandable for Mr. Darcy to challenge Mr. Wickham. Perhaps I should add one in a future novel. Perhaps include a gloomy abbey. Might as well."

"Shhh." Joan speared them all with a glare.

Soon the comfort of Marco's presence and the familiar score had Wren's lids drooping. When she woke, the living room was silent. Pale light filtered in through the slats of the blinds. Her head was on Marco's shoulder and his arm lay draped across her shoulders in a sleepy embrace. Someone had put the throw over the two of them. She sighed, happily. Cozy and warm, it was all she could do not to snuggle deeper into her little happy cocoon.

Marco stirred and stretched. "Morning."

"Already?" Wren shivered at the sudden absence of his arm from her shoulders.

"Guess so." He gave her a sleepy shrug, then leaned forward to crack his back. She cursed the daylight.

Joan rolled over, shattering the bubble that Wren was actually alone with Marco. Wren blinked. Part of her had hoped the three visitors would stay asleep longer so she could have more uninterrupted time with him.

"Shhh. You'll wake the others," Wren said. She gestured to the snoring Jane under a blanket on the floor. Joan slept next to her and had wrapped the bottom of her legs to her waist in a checkered shawl, the rubber sword clutched tightly to her chest, the sword Wren would somehow have to get backstage again. And Elvis lay sprawled on a chair, finally relaxed. The man kept mentioning how terrifying it'd be to fall asleep and then awaken somewhere, not knowing how he'd gotten there. It'd taken a bit of coaxing, and the help of some melatonin gummies, to convince him that no sleepwalking would happen while he drifted off to dreamland.

"What do you think, should I put my hair in a pompadour for the play tonight?" Marco twirled his front locks and leaned back against the sofa.

"Might upstage the other lead," Wren quipped. The other lead played Lady Amelia, Marco's onstage love interest, who Marco had once admitted looked cute in the pastel pink empire waist dress Wren had picked out for the part. Tonight, he'd hold her in his arms and kiss her onstage.

"I can't be responsible for doing that to Lady Amelia and her exotic bird wig." He laughed, then sobered.

"Hey, I know you've chosen to be the amazing costumier and props manager this troupe has. I'm impressed you're skilled enough to do both, honestly. But you're not the only one who gets stage fright," Marco said.

"Don't patronize me." What, would he be scared of kissing a cute woman onstage now? The vision of the two actors practicing the part over and over again did nothing for her growing jealousy.

Elvis rose and shuffled toward the kitchen. Jane yawned, sitting up. Great. She and Marco were having their talk right then, in front of the strangers. Anxiety began to color her envy.

"Wren, I feel it in my feet and then it works its way up to my hands and mouth if I don't conquer it." He searched her face. "All I'm saying is, I get it."

Studying him, the earnestness in his gaze, she let go of her bad mood. "Thanks."

"I know you love the props and costumes, but," he bumped her shoulder with his, "don't use it to hide either." He brushed a lock of her red curls behind an ear. "You're so multitalented. Reconsider being the understudy tonight. Or at least, consider possibly doing the next play and taking a break from the wardrobe workroom and backstage wings."

"I don't know. You're sweet, but I know what you're trying to do. I just don't have time to delve into my phobias today. And with opening night, I have some last-minute fixes for the costumes and all."

He sighed. "Sure. Later then."

Chapter Six

After a quick breakfast of peanut butter and banana toast —no bacon, much to Elvis's disappointment—Wren was back at the theater.

She threw herself into readying the costumes and props for the performance. Jane and Joan had peppered her with questions while she'd put them to work. Joan polished any swords or armor in the prop room. Jane read through the script and then helped with the fraying hems of a few gowns. Looking up from a frothy yellow dress she'd been mending, Jane sighed.

"What?" Wren asked.

"I was only considering the scene you and your friend Marco acted last night. If that was a mere sample of tonight's play, then I fear this performance will have more holes in the story than a piece of muslin the mice had gotten into."

Joan snorted from her corner where she was polishing the silverware, a pile of gleaming weapons and armor at her feet.

"Nothing to do about it now," Wren mused. "The director wants what he wants. Weird phrasing, bad plots, and all."

"But the ending," Jane continued. "I had to know and asked Mr. Manzanares. I simply do not understand why Lady Amelia would go to a ball while her own sister, Katherine, was ill. Would she not be concerned about her sibling the entire night? We never see Katherine later in the play. Does she recover? Or does she succumb to her illness?"

"I don't know." Wren stuck her needle into the straw bonnet ribbon, securing it in place. The mention of Lady Amelia irked her more than she wanted to admit. "Look, there isn't a Katherine that goes onstage. She's just mentioned in the dialogue."

Jane scoffed. "Then that is a cut that needs doing. And I fear, your director needs my prompt attention."

"You can't," Wren said.

"And why ever not? It is a chance to change something for the better. You do not realize the luxury you have in your time. I am a woman of a period where it is shameful to even publish one's own name to a novel. Instead, I must hide behind anonymity. 'By A Lady' is no author. It is cowardice. You, dear, have no need for being anonymous. Why, you can even act onstage without bringing disgrace to your family."

"If only I could." Wren stabbed the fabric at the collar of the gown she was repairing and clinked the needle against the thimble on her forefinger.

"I cannot change the constraints set on myself and other women put out by the government and the *ton*, but here, now, you have none but yourself that keeps you in check," Jane said.

She stood, handing the finished yellow gown to Wren. "I shall be gone but a small while. And when I return, I will be victorious."

Joan cheered, waving the polishing cloth like a pennant above her head. Wren sat in shock. Jane Austen had just chastised her. And, dare she say it, pitied her for not being more courageous.

Twenty minutes to curtain, Marco came to the costume room. "Got a minute?" he asked.

"What happened? Is it the wigs? I told Elvis to leave them alone."

Marco laughed. "No. Look, about earlier today...it's all—"

"Big problem." The assistant director walked into the costume room, phone in hand. She cast a panicked look at the two of them. "Our Lady Amelia's sick. And there's no understudy."

"She's only the female lead." Wren grimaced. "No one would notice her being written out, right?"

That earned her a glare.

"It's sold out," the assistant director said. "I'm not going out there to tell everyone to go home."

"Wren, it's a sign," Marco said. "You know the lines. Be our Lady Amelia."

The assistant director looked at her. "You'd do it?"

"We literally went over the hardest part last night." Marco grabbed Wren's hands and looked her in the eyes. The jolt she'd felt before returned to settle in her middle. "We could be the best Lord Steffington and Lady Amelia. I know you can do it. Please?"

Nearly paralyzed, her breathing quickened. Her pulse raced. On stage, under those lights, in front of the audience, in a role she'd never played before in her life while fighting dry heaves. She couldn't. "I'm sorry."

"I get it." He dropped her hands and stepped back. "Didn't mean to pressure you."

There, right before his fake smile, was a flash of disappointment. He left the costume room. A knife wound would've felt better than knowing she'd hurt her best friend.

The assistant director sighed. "Get a replacement into costume ASAP."

Wren waited until the door slammed behind her before she let out a breath.

"You know it has to be you," came a calm voice at her side. Joan.

"I'll just ruin it for Marco."

"Psh. Why are you so afraid?" Joan asked. "What is there to lose?"

"I don't expect you to understand. You're not afraid of anything."

Joan placed her hands on Wren's shoulders. "*Au contraire, mon amie.* I am afraid every day of my life," she said, her face close to Wren's. "But I know, inside, I was born to fight anyway. Use your fear and be stronger for it. Think of the theater. Think of Marco."

Wren stared at the young woman before her. A teenager had more courage than she had.

"The company will do fine without me." Defeat already colored Wren's voice. "I'd just freeze up there."

Hands pressed on either side of Wren's face, squishing her lips. "*Mon amie*, prove them wrong. Your name means—"

"Songbird. But I can't sing."

"*Non*, it means 'queen.' Act like one. Own the stage in all its glory." Joan let go. "*Courage!*" she shouted, then left the costume room. Wren took a deep breath.

Chapter Seven

Ten minutes later, dressed in a burgundy coat over a gold cotton empire-waist gown, Wren paced backstage. She did not wear the wig. Besides, Jane had said it was "so last season." She'd also told her to nix Katherine from the script entirely. Wren's nerves bunched as she waited behind the masking curtains, mentally repeating the new lines. She smoothed the front of her coat with trembling fingers. She could do this. She had to.

"You're gonna be great tonight," Elvis said, next to her. "Practice with me. 'Chop shops stock chops.' Say it three times. And then we do the Judo Dragon breath." He kicked the air and exhaled loudly.

"Shhh," Wren said. "You'll get us in trouble."

"Nah, honey. You gotta do it. Loosen the shoulders at least," he whispered.

Wren shrugged them up and down a few times then stared at him. He crossed his arms and pressed his lips together. *Fine,* she mouthed.

"Chop shops stock chops. Chop shops." It was stupid. And it sounded so ridiculous in a whisper. "Stock chops. Happy?"

"Now the kick and punch," Elvis whispered.

"On in two," a stagehand said.

The set change was coming up and then Lady Amelia was supposed to faint dead away on the couch. Her first appearance to the audience before the intermission. The backstage crew silently placed the furniture on the stage, one person running in to throw a shawl on the sofa at the last second. The front curtain rose. A loud clank of the spotlights echoed in the silent audience as all waited for the performance to continue.

"And go," the stagehand said.

Wren's heart beat out of rhythm. Her throat went dry.

"You're on."

One beat. Two.

"Honey, they're waiting for you. Show them what you're made of." Elvis hip-swiveled, bumping her forward into the lights.

Beyond the blaze of white, she could make out hundreds of round dark blobs in the audience.

Marco waltzed onto the stage. His pale blue and gold frock coat glimmered in the spotlight as he paused, the only sign of his shock. "Is that you, Lady Amelia?"

She glanced at him. "Indeed, it is I."

"Ah, but what a fine day it must be to have your presence, if only for a few hours."

What was her line? Her eyes opened wide. It was happening again.

"And if I am not mistaken, you would love to spend that time with me," Marco prompted, coming closer.

Every breath was a struggle. Every instinct told her to run. Exit, stage left. But her feet remained firmly planted to the floor.

"Lord Steffington, you mistake my silence for approval," Jane whispered loudly from the side.

Wren repeated the new line. A true improvisation now. That wasn't in the script. Marco's eyebrows flicked upward just slightly. The audience began to laugh. What had they done? The audience wasn't supposed to laugh then. It was a serious part in the play. There was a warm pressure on her hand.

"Eyes on me," Marco whispered. Her eyes met his and she took comfort in his faith in her. He smiled broadly, his cheeks two bright pink painted circles under his over-the-top powdered wig. Wren looked away, pretending to be bashful. Buying time.

"Ah, but approval you give anyway," Jane whispered again, pinning Marco with a glance this time.

Marco hid his flub with a small chuckle then stated his new line. He dropped Wren's hands.

"Shall we escape the confines of the room and take a turn around the garden, my dear sweet cabbage blossom? I fear the light in your complexion is paling in this gloom." His eyes crinkled as he spoke, and Wren laughed. "Have you tried the remedy of sliced potatoes most recently?"

"Cabbage? Potatoes?" she managed between a giggle. The tension broken, she remembered where they were in the script and quickly pushed his hand away. "My goodness, Lord Steffington, it seems you think me but a quaint country garden." She sashayed away, untying her bonnet but choking herself in the process. The audience laughed again.

"Use your fear," Jane said once more from backstage. Jane Austen poured her fear, her every ounce of everything, into not only her works, but her life. Maybe she couldn't write under her own name in her lifetime, but she'd written novels, nevertheless. Jane had even gone to their own director, in the modern day, to change the script. She persevered, even when nothing seemed to go her way. Wren stood taller.

"On second thought, perhaps a garden would gain better attention from this man," Wren spoke as an aside to the audience. She feigned a fainting fit and proceeded to fall toward the sofa but miscalculated the distance. She fell to the floor with a loud thud, skirts askew. Tears stung her eyes but not as much as the sting of silence from the audience.

"*Courage*," she heard from the wings.

"My sweet butter bean!" Marco was by her side in seconds. He sought her face. "Pray, are you hurt?"

Thinking quickly, she turned her head to the audience and gave an exaggerated wink. A few chuckles came from the back of the theater, and then a couple more. Perfect. "Oh, oh, Lord Steffington, I fear we shall have to forgo the ball tonight."

"Let me put your concern at rest. For I shall attend to your every need." The quirk of his lips, the crinkle at the corner of his eyes. How Marco managed to say it with a straight face, Wren never knew. But there was one thing she did know. It was now or never.

Placing a hand behind his neck, she pulled his face toward hers. Nerves fluttered around like possessed butterflies inside her as her lips met his. Warmth flooded her cheeks to nestle deep within her. She drew back.

Marco blinked under the lights.

As the silence wore on unbearably, she spoke. "My Lord, have I rendered you speechless?" then dropped to a whisper. "Too soon?"

He shook his head, a smile spreading his lips. "Not soon enough," he said and drew her into another kiss onstage.

The curtain dropped.

The backstage crew whooped as the audience clapped. A warm breeze blew the nape of her neck and Wren looked to the wings in time to see Jane, Joan, and Elvis wave before the trio disappeared in a cloud of blue smoke.

Marco helped Wren up, and they rushed offstage before the stage manager yelled at them.

"Where'd they go?" Marco asked, glancing around.

"Home, I think. Their part in this is done after all."

"What do you mean?" he asked.

"They came for us. To get us to finally admit our feelings." She smiled as he took her hand. "But there's one thing that bugs me. When I made that wish for love and courage, I know why Jane and Joan came, but I don't understand why Elvis did."

"Don't hate me..." Marco flushed. "I might've wished on your candles."

Her jaw dropped. "You're not supposed to wish on other people's birthday cakes." Then she began to chuckle. "It must not have been a very strong wish since all you got was Elvis. Aside from eating you out of peanut butter and teaching me to judo chop, he wasn't much help at all."

"I beg to differ, my little radish sprout. He was the one that kept encouraging me to keep trying and gave me the confidence I needed to tell my best friend I like her." His blush deepened, matching his painted cheeks. "Still friends?"

She considered him a second. "No."

"No?" A crease formed between his dark brows.

"More."

"More...cupcakes?" he asked, his thumb circling the back of her hand.

Wren nodded.

"More...movie nights?" He raised a brow.

She smiled at him, nodding slowly.

"More..." He paused, licking his lips. "Waking up with you in my arms?"

"Yes please." She tugged the lapel of his frock coat to her. "I want all of it. But those red fuzzy handcuffs...?"

"You know about those?" His eyes flew wide.

"Very interesting choice. You know, you shouldn't let just anyone in your room. Never know what they might discover. Or use against you."

"You wouldn't dare," he growled in her ear before kissing her soundly.

Just before Wren's thoughts turned to pudding, she thought she heard Marco whisper, "Thank you. Thank you very much."

Author's Note

~

Researching for this story was a job in and of itself, and one I truly enjoyed. It started with a Sci Fi anthology prompt where I had to "take any three famous people from history, toss them together, and have an adventure." The story grew from there and *voilà!*

"Why the theater? Why Jane and Joan and Elvis?" you might ask. And I'd have to counter with, why not?

You know the whole "write what you know" adage... I used some of my own experiences of performing onstage in musicals and high school plays with the Staples Players and St. John's Singers. Ghosts in the wings have always been a delightful mystery amongst the performers. But what if those ghosts weren't ghosts, but flesh and blood, having traveled with a mission...

Jane Austen has been a favorite historical figure of mine since I read *Pride and Prejudice* in the tenth grade in Mr. Russey's English class. The author fascinated me. Her wit, her way with words, her ability to bring to life the everyday in a not so everyday way— I could go on much longer than you probably have patience for.

Yet, there is a lot surrounding her life that is still left to be discovered. In this work, I focused on some classic visuals to place her in the minds of my readers, but what was compelling to me was the fact that along with her sparkling mind, she was considered quite a beauty.

Jane Austen's favorite nephew, James Edward Austen Leigh, described her in his memoir, *Memoir of Jane Austen*, as "very attractive; her figure was rather tall and slender, her step light and firm, and her whole appearance expressive of health and animation. In complexion she was a clear brunette with a rich colour; she had full round cheeks, with mouth and nose small and well formed, bright hazel eyes, and brown hair forming natural curls close round her face." (Austen Leigh, 1870, p. 87)

I took those descriptions, combined with the famous portrait done by her sister Cassandra, and the wit she was known for, and created my version of who I believe Jane Austen would've been. If I am wrong in my assumptions, I apologize.

Joan of Arc, Jeanne d'Arc, or Jehanne D'Arc, was harder. Although there is almost no physical image of her, save for a line drawing made by a person recording her victory of freeing Orleans— a drawing based on his idea of her, having never seen or met her in real life, mind you— my research gave me a few things to go off of. Most of her physical descriptions came from descriptions in writings.

She was pretty short, about five-foot-two to be exact, based on the request from the Duke of Orleans that a measure of cloth be bought to make a robe for her. She had dark hair that was kept short, likely cut in the male pudding-basin or pageboy fashion of the time. She had large, dark, serious eyes. She possibly had a red birthmark behind her right ear (I didn't include that). She was described as sturdy, muscular, and tanned from being outside so much and working fields with her family. And she was very passionate in her beliefs. She also had a quick temper.

I read that during her trials, a clerical examiner, who spoke in a heavy accent, had asked her what language the voices in her head spoke. Without missing a beat, she replied that the voices spoke French better than he did!

Knowing this and knowing her fondness for military garb and weapons, though she'd never killed anyone and preferred her banner to swords, I developed my Joan character. I did my best not to take too many liberties, but as an author, sometimes they must happen. To my knowledge, no one has had Joan of Arc time travel to help them yet.

And then there was Elvis Presley. Marco requested the ultimate someone who was the King of Charisma for him, and I couldn't deny my hero. Who else could it be but The King, himself?

He was a lot of fun to write. I focused on the more known traits of Elvis, like his love of peanut butter, and soul food. His humble beginnings sure shaped his tastes as he grew up. His cook, Mary Jenkins Langston, made everything for him and usually brought it up to him in bed. His favorite, aside from the peanut butter and banana sandwiches, the Fool's Gold (look that one up!), and barbecue, was breakfast food.

There's a nod to the movie, "Jailhouse Rock," where he had to shoot scenes offering popcorn to an actress, but not eat it. Trivia factoid: his favorite movie-watching snack was popcorn, Pepsi, and SweetTarts dropped into it. And he liked to be right in the middle of the theater.

I also tried to include lots of nods to his love of the martial arts. It wasn't judo, but karate Elvis was known for, having a black belt and then receiving an honorary eighth degree black belt rank weeks before he died.

Wren was wrong about him in the book and I kept it, showing her confusion about why he was there. Elvis was perfect for the role, but that's my humble opinion.

As for the time travel aspect, I chose a more magical, mythical way of portraying it, instead of the more sci-fi version with lots of science. I decided against a portal and instead chose smoke, a more magical and mystical entrance. It felt right with the theater, emphasizing the unknown and ghosts and time travelers.

But blue smoke you ask? Well, yeah! Because the color blue in color theory represents competence, trust, peace, and loyalty. I thought it fitting with the appearance of the "muses" for Wren.

And there you have it, the insider's knowledge of this novelette. Hope you enjoyed it!

Lots of love,
Erin Krueger

Acknowledgments

~

First off, thank you, dear readers, for picking up my book and taking a chance on a new author. My biggest hope is that my work brought a smile to your face, some fun to your day, and perhaps a bit of courage to pursue your dreams.

I'd like to thank The Red Reines who encouraged me to dig deep, and deeper still, and push myself with writing.

Specifically, Carol Potenza, for her amazing critique and scholarly knowledge of all things science and history related; Jordyn Kross, who nailed me on plot holes and better word choices; and Ryley Banks, whose critiques were invaluable with a touch of humor and preliminary editing, and who also nudged me in a not-so-gentle way to submit my work to a sci-fi short story contest specializing in time travel.

Amy Paulussen, my Kiwi beta reader, who made me expand in places where it needed more faff and ruthlessly cut where it was unremarkable.

My gifted and wonderfully talented cover artist, Brandi Doane, whose work is nothing short of magical, THANK YOU.

My editor, Alyssa Krueger, who shall forever be my Comma Queen and bearer of chuckles at the misfortune of spellcheck not recognizing Elvis Presley's name.

My son, Ronan, who slept long naps on the days I needed to write, revise, and edit.

My dog Mochi, who kept me company and guarded my office door while I worked midnight edits, the best author pet anyone could have.

My husband, Brendan Krueger. The countless cups of coffee when I needed the energy, the listening ear as I worked out plots and paced from my office to our kitchen and back again, the support and confidence in me that helped me keep going, and the many, many read throughs of rough drafts and revisions of the story...words really can't convey the depths of all I feel. So I'll keep it simple. I love you, honey. Thank you for believing in me.

And last but not least, Jane Austen, my first literary love. Jehanne D'Arc, whose history brought new light to my mind. And Elvis Presley, who still remains The King in my mind.

Without all these folks, this novelette would not have been distilled out of the barest hint of ether and onto the pages to be read.

About the Author

Erin Krueger writes historic time travel romance, small town contemporary romance, and self-help nonfiction.

She's been an analytical chemist in New York, a treasurer for New Mexico romance writers, an au pair and ex-pat in France, a connoisseur of peppermint ice cream in Sweden, an amateur photographer of almond trees in Spain, and a wanderer of castles in Britain. Finding the secret romantic places couples centuries before her have visited is one of her favorite pastimes.

Northern New Mexico is home, shared with her husband, son, and rescue dog. As far as Erin knows, she's not related to the fiendish 80s villain with the same last name, but the DNA's still being processed. Should you need to find her, look for the largest cup of tea or coffee possible. She's usually nearby!

facebook.com/ErinKruegerWrites

instagram.com/erinkruegerwrites

bookbub.com/profile/erin-krueger

goodreads.com/erinkruegerwrites

Erin's Brew Crew

Scan the QR code above or go to erinkruegerwrites.com to sign up for Erin's VIP Brew Crew monthly newsletter.

It's the only spot where you'll get her latest writing updates, release news, quirky history facts and fascinating recipes, freebies, book recs, and more!

Also by Erin Krueger

Scan the QR code or go to

https://erinkruegerwrites.com/books/

<u>*Fiction*</u>

<u>Khaki and Lace</u> *A Designers in Time Series Book 1*

Coming soon!

"Time Will Tell" *A Designers in Time Short Story*

<u>*Nonfiction*</u>

<u>Demystifying the Beats: How to Write a Killer Book</u> by Carol Potenza, Jordyn Kross, Ryley Banks, and Erin Krueger

Read More: Time Will Tell (excerpt)

A DESIGNERS IN TIME SHORT STORY

ERIN KRUEGER

Time Will Tell (excerpt)

In a stale and ostentatious lecture hall in Prague, Susan shifted on her seat, the dark floorboards beneath her creaking with the sudden imbalance of weight. For a rich velvet cushion, it was decidedly uncomfortable and hard. Dr. Dannington, attired in an innocuous faded tweed coat with brown leather elbow patches, his round golden glasses perched at the end of his nose, droned on and on and *on* about the treasures of the past.

Treasures. What a joke. The man seemed to find joy in making her suffer.

Who cared about the rocking horse Teddy Roosevelt rode on as a toddler? Or the stories antique dishes could tell? The tiny mourning locket with a snipping of a spouse's hair from some insignificant woman? Nostalgic nonsense like that made her eyes cross.

Seriously, what significance did the study of antique LEGO or novelty lava lamps hold for the present or future populations? One word: none.

Susan sat up straighter, her lips curving into a small smile. What mattered *most*—what her genius mentor had sacrificed everything for in that fated travel last month—was—

"The absence of Dr. Rippolini is most regrettable at our gathering. However, we are graced with her mentee, a re-established member of the Society of Travelers, Dr. Susan Barrows."

The hall echoed in applause and Dannington ushered her forward to the podium, leading her by the elbow. He leaned in close and spoke in her ear.

"Now, we don't want a repeat offense like we did the last time you presented. Do keep that in mind. I would hate for anything...untoward to happen to you should you decide to spread more of your heretical ideas." He gestured to the side of the stage, where shadows of muscular goons lurked just out of the light. They stood, their gazes laser-focused on her. "Your choice," he said with a shrug and walked off.

Susan dropped her notecards on top of the dark stained podium and took a steadying breath, ignoring the blatant threat.

"Thank you, fellow scientists, colleagues, Dr. Dannington." She nodded to the man who'd introduced her, the sole acknowledgement he deserved. He'd been behind her first banishment. Then the society was *oh so kind* to write to her last month to let her back in. As if they were going against their better judgement.

Her ideas had been so brilliant, they'd *had* to let her back in. And her mere presence, with a reinstated membership, was a one-fingered salute to all who controlled the narrative.

Dannington.

"It is indeed an honor to be able to present to you my thrilling new research of historical importance: Tangible History." Still, there was hope that they'd listen, see the value. Her years of hard work and calculated planning would pay off. "Tangible History. What is it exactly? It's a way to experience the *important* moments of the past in a firsthand manner."

"Here it comes, again," someone muttered from the front row. It was followed by a few harrumphs of agreement in the audience. Always the rebel, Susan wasn't there to placate the masses. She forced a smile and continued.

"Experience, by way of simple observation, will be key. Nothing done to change the course of events. I'm sure we're all aware of the traveler rule of thumb. The longer one is there, the more the river of time will force you out. With our invention, the traveler, with a keen mind and the proper training, will be able to slip through time quickly, witness Bell's first telephone call, Herschel's comet discovery, or the *exact* moment Newton came up with gravity, then slip out again and be free to draw the correct conclusions of their significance, and by turn, the impor-tance of the event for the present and future."

That was the key to Susan's research. Why would anyone prefer to hold onto a flawed memory or story in history? Certainly not her, child of divorced parents, made to grow up with the liar. People could hold onto their rose-colored pasts all they liked. Susan craved the truth. Others deserved the same.

"Imagine if you will, a graduate student, from an unknown university, researching a paper and having the ability to go back to a precise moment of discovery. They can draw their own conclusions of the success of the invention, observe antiques and relics as a *direct observer*, saving valuable time and energy. Then contrast that with what we have now, with historians assimilating written words from say, the Prussian War, and what is known about the culture at the time, postulating present and future narratives that could be erroneous. *Filtered* facts based on who is allowed to filter it. The victors?" She took stock of the audience, seats filled with members of an exclusive society, the aristocracy of science in most cases, sponsored by government funding. Her blood seethed beneath her skin.

"Who decides what is 'misinformation?' Those who control the narrative." Her thoughts shot again to Dr. Rippolini. How her mentor was *controlled* in the last mission. "So elitist. So dictatorial. So...fearful." She leveled her gaze at the hall. "Do away with the filtration and what's left? Truth."

Some members made a show of leaving their seats and walking out of the lecture hall. She'd struck a nerve. Good. History needed to be written correctly. Rewrite the books. Heck, maybe books would be obsolete soon. They were, after all, written by the winners, an unbalanced portrayal of events, not recording both sides.

"With Tangible History, it's not up to the top scientists and historians what is labeled as information and misinformation. Instead of gatekeepers, the everyman will be capable of determining that for themselves."

Out of the corner of her vision she saw Dannington step closer to her. A prickle of alarm worked its way down her arms.

"But what of the dangers of time travel?" A voice dared to interrupt her.

Susan narrowed her eyes, trying to find the source.

Third row. Center seat.

The scientist sat with his arms crossed, lips pressed together in false disbelief. Dr. Kurtis.

"Dangers?" she asked, not hiding the sneer from her lips. She'd been waiting for a question from one of Dannington's sycophants.

With a smug expression on his pompous face, an arrogant tilt of his head, and steepled fingers, Kurtis spoke again.

"I was asking about the effects of time travel on the human body. Surely, you're not claiming there isn't a toll on somebody somewhere. A body part could go missing." A pin dropping would have sounded like a bomb in the silent hall.

"I understood you. I was merely trying to comprehend why you'd bring up the question when just in last month's society serial there was a paper that reported on the studies of the harmless nature of time travel. I see that information may not have been given to all. A gatekeeping measure. For shame. No, on the missions conducted, there haven't been any issues with the human body. No fingers went missing in the travel. Not a scratch on an arm. Not a hair came back mussed. Our portal doors to the past or future are just that, a doorway. Nothing to hurt the human." Susan flicked at a speck of dust on her sleeve.

"I see. But isn't it true that Dr. Rippolini never returned from the last mission?"

Susan's hand froze, mid swipe...

IF YOU'D LIKE to find out the conclusion to Time Will Tell, a free Designers in Time Short Story, scan the QR code and sign up for Erin's Brew Crew!

Or go to Time Will Tell on Erin's website and sign up for her newsletter there!